W9-BYL-749

Fairy Realm

Book 5

The Magic Key

Fairy Realm

The Magic Key

Book 5

EMILY RODDA

ILLUSTRATIONS BY RAOUL VITALE

HARPERCOLLINSPUBLISHERS

visit us at www.abdopublishing.com

Reinforced library bound edition published in 2008 by Spotlight, a division of the ABDO Publishing Group, Edina, Minnesota. Published by agreement with HarperCollins Children's Books.

Previously published by ABC Books for the AUSTRALIAN BROADCASTING CORPORATION GPO Box 9994 Sydney NSW 2001
Originally published under the name
Mary-Anne Dickinson as the Storytelling Charms Series 1995

Library of Congress Cataloging-in-Publication Data
Rodda, Emily.
The magic key / Emily Rodda ; illustrations by Raoul Vitale.
p. cm. -- (Fairy realm ; bk. 5)
"Originally published under the name Mary-Anne Dickinson as the Storytelling Charms Series, 1995."
Sequel to: The last fairy-apple tree.
Sequel: The unicorn.
Summary: On her fifth journey to the magical Fairy Realm, Jessie, this time on her birthday, travels all the way to the end of the rainbow and tries to help her new friends, the rainbow fairies.
ISBN-13: 978-1-59961-327-7 (reinforced library bound edition)
ISBN-10: 1-59961-327-1 (reinforced library bound edition)
[1. Fairies--Fiction. 2. Rainbow--Fiction. 3. Birthdays--Fiction. 4. Magic--Fiction.] I. Vitale, Raoul, ill. II. Title.
PZ7.R5996Mag 2007
[Fic]--dc22 2006021986

All Spotlight books are reinforced library binding
and manufactured in the United States of America

CONTENTS

Fairy Realm

BOOK 5

The Magic Key

CHAPTER ONE

Rain, Rain, Go Away

When Jessie woke up on the day of her birthday party, it was raining.

"Oh no!" she groaned. She slid out of bed and went to look out the window.

"Rain, rain, go away, come again another day," she chanted.

But the rain kept falling.

Everything was dark and dripping. The sky was heavy and gray. The red and orange leaves on the trees drooped. Many had fallen to the ground. The flowers hung their heads. The birds were all hidden away.

Now the party would have to be held inside, instead of outside. They wouldn't be able to play any of the games Jessie had planned.

The Blue Moon garden was so beautiful, with its enormous old trees, overgrown winding paths, and hidden corners. Jessie had been sure her friends would enjoy the party, whatever Irena Bins thought.

She'd overheard Irena talking to a girl called Amy Peel at school on Friday. Friday had been Jessie's real birthday. And it had been a beautiful sunny day, Jessie remembered. Whoever would have thought the weather could change so fast?

"Oh, yes, I'm going to Jessie's party," Irena had said, in a loud drawling voice. "I sort of have to, you know? Because I live next door. But you're lucky you're not, Amy, honestly. It's going to be really *boring*. No magician or videos or anything. Just little kids' games in the yard."

"Don't take any notice of her," Jessie's friend Sal had whispered in her ear. "She's only saying all that because she knows you're listening. She just wants to hurt your feelings. She's a pig."

Jessie had pretended she didn't care. But she did, of course. And now she felt her face grow hot as she remembered the rest of what Irena had said.

"Do you know, Jessie's not even going to have a new *dress* for the party?" she'd gone on, lowering her voice very slightly. "Mum says her mother probably can't afford one. She's just a nurse at the hospital."

Then Amy had said something and Irena had shaken her head scornfully.

"That huge old Blue Moon place isn't theirs." She'd sniffed. "Jessie and her mother have just lived there since they moved up from the city. It belongs to Jessie's grandmother. Jessie's grandfather was a painter. Made all this money painting crazy pictures of fairies and elves and stuff."

Jessie had stared straight ahead as the low, spiteful voice chattered on.

"He's dead now, but Mrs. Belairs, Jessie's grandmother, still lives at Blue Moon. And, boy, wait till the other kids meet *her*."

"What's the matter with her?" Amy had asked curiously.

"She's really *weird*," Irena had whispered. "Talks to her cat as if it's a person. Keeps her clothes done up with safety pins. Acts like a little kid half the time. When it rains, she purposely goes outside and walks around getting soaked. Dad says she's batty."

"Shut up, Irena," Sal had shouted, glancing at Jessie's hurt face in concern. "You shut *up*!"

But Irena had just raised her eyebrows, tossed her hair back, and stared at Sal with wide-open eyes.

"What's wrong with *you*?" she'd said.

Then she'd gone off with Amy, giggling and whispering, and looking back over her shoulder at Jessie and Sal.

Remembering, Jessie gritted her teeth. She didn't really care what Irena had said about her not having a new party dress. But she *did* care what she'd said about her party—and about Granny.

Sometimes Jessie almost wished that the Bins family would find out Granny's secret. She almost wished they'd find out just how unusual her grandmother really was. Then they'd get a shock!

What would they say if they knew that Jessie's grandfather hadn't painted things he'd made up, but things he'd actually *seen*? What would they say if they knew that Granny was not from this world at all?

What would they say if they knew she was the rightful Queen of the fairy world called the Realm? That she'd left it when she was young to marry the human man she loved, leaving her sister Helena to rule in her place?

Jessie had always known that her grandmother was special.

She'd always loved Blue Moon, Granny's old house in the mountains, even before she came to live there.

But she'd never forget the day she discovered the invisible Door at the bottom of Granny's garden, and entered the Realm for the first time. Ever since then, her life had been filled with adventure.

Sometimes, when she hadn't visited the Realm for a while, it almost seemed to Jessie that it was a dream. But then she'd look at the charm bracelet on her wrist.

Each charm that hung on the bracelet had been a gift from the Realm. Memories flooded back whenever Jessie looked at the charms shining golden against her skin.

Memories came into her mind now, as she turned from the window. She smiled, thinking of her Realm friends: Maybelle the miniature horse, Giff the elf, and Patrice, the palace housekeeper. She thought of Queen Helena, too, and all the other fairy people and creatures she'd met.

She wished she could see them today. She wished she could go down to the still, secret garden hidden behind the hedge, go through the magic Door, and disappear into the Realm.

But she knew she couldn't. It was the day of her birthday party. Rain or no rain, she had to be at Blue Moon to meet her friends this afternoon.

Shaking her head, she pulled on some jeans and an old top, and wandered out to the kitchen.

Granny was there, sitting at the table and drinking a cup of tea. Her big ginger cat, Flynn, purred at her feet. Jessie saw that Granny's hair was damp and her cheeks were pink.

She's been out in the garden, wandering around in the rain again, Jessie thought. I hope the Bins didn't see her.

"Hello, Jessie," Granny said. Her bright green eyes twinkled as she smiled. "Birthday party day."

Jessie flopped into a chair. "And it's raining!" she groaned. "Can you believe it?"

"I suppose I have to." Granny laughed, looking through the kitchen window at the rain pattering down. "But never mind. All will be well. Won't it, Flynn?"

Flynn meowed, and lifted his chin to be scratched.

"We won't be able to play in the garden now," Jessie said. "We'll have to stay inside, and everyone will get bored."

And everything Irena Bins said will come true, she thought. She sighed heavily.

Granny put her head on one side.

"Have some breakfast," she suggested. "Don't worry. Look on the bright side."

"What bright side is there to look on?" demanded Jessie.

Granny shrugged. "Rain makes everything in the garden grow. And after rain, everything's fresh and clean. Lots of things love the rain. Pixies, for example."

She smiled. "And don't forget, Jessie—if it wasn't for rain there wouldn't be rainbows. No beautiful colors in the sky. No pot of gold. And no rainbow fairies."

Jessie loved the story of the pot of fairy gold at the end of the rainbow.

Her grandfather, Robert Belairs, had painted quite a few rainbows. In his paintings a glimmer of gold always lit the ground at the rainbow's end. And in the glimmer moved slim shapes with wings. Rainbow fairies.

"I haven't seen a rainbow fairy for a long, long time," said Granny, stroking Flynn. "The young ones often used to come to the secret garden, to watch the rainbows in the sprinklers. I loved to see them. But they seem to have stopped visiting now. I wonder why."

"Maybe they're too busy minding their pots of gold," Jessie said.

"There's more than just a pot of gold at the end of the rainbow, you know," Granny told her. "There's always a Door to the Realm, too. If you find the rainbow's end you have to choose. The gold, or a visit to the Realm. Most people take the gold."

"They're crazy, then," said Jessie.

"I suppose they don't know what they're missing. And maybe a pot of gold *is* more useful."

"But—" Jessie began. Then she stopped short and looked at her grandmother sideways. "You're trying to make me argue, to take my mind off the rain!" she accused her.

"Of course!" Granny laughed. "I don't want you glooming around all miserable."

"I know," Jessie said. "And I don't mind the rain usually. I just wish it wasn't raining *today*."

"Today will still be a lovely day for you, Jessie," said Granny. "I've been thinking about it."

Jessie looked up at her. "About how to stop the rain?" she asked hopefully.

"No." Granny poured herself another cup of tea. "Not how to stop the rain. I still have some powers. Quite useful powers, too. But controlling the weather isn't one of them."

Jessie looked down at the tabletop.

"What I've been thinking about," Granny said cheerfully, "is how to make the best of what we have. How to make sure everyone has a good time, even in the rain."

Jessie forced a smile and nodded.

"And of course the rain might easily stop—all by itself," Granny went on. "It's still very early. Your friends won't be here till three o'clock. That's hours and hours away! Anything might happen."

Jessie doubted it. But still, she felt a bit better. Somehow Granny was always able to make things seem brighter. She made herself a bowl of cereal and fruit, and started to eat.

"Your mother should be home soon," said Granny, looking at the clock on the wall. "Poor Rosemary, she'll be tired. This night duty is hard on her."

"She'll be wet, too," Jessie said with her mouth full. "She didn't take an umbrella or anything with her last night."

"Ah, well," Granny said comfortably. "A little bit of water never hurt anyone. You can soon dry off. I like a walk in the rain myself. It's fun."

"That's one of the reasons why the Bins think you're crazy, Granny," Jessie pointed out.

Granny sniffed. "What do I care what those boring Bins think? They wouldn't know a good time if they fell over it. Why on earth did you invite Irena to the party, Jessie?"

"Mum made me," said Jessie. "Because Irena lives next door. Mum didn't want to hurt her feelings."

Granny sniffed again. "That girl doesn't *have* any feelings, if you ask me."

Flynn arched his back and meowed loudly. Obviously he agreed.

After a few minutes Jessie heard the sound of her mother's car in the driveway. Granny ran out with an umbrella, and soon Rosemary herself was in the room with them. Her eyes were red with tiredness, and her nurse's uniform was soaked through.

"I can't believe this rain!" She gasped. "I got

drenched just running from the hospital to my car. And, oh, Jessie! Your birthday party! I'm so sorry!"

"It'll be all right, Mum," said Jessie quickly.

"Yes. All will be well, Rosemary," said Granny. "Now you go and have a nice hot shower and get into your dressing gown. I'll make you some breakfast and then you can have a sleep. You've been up all night. You need to rest."

"But what about the party?" Rosemary protested weakly. "We'll have to make some new arrangements, now it's raining. Think up some new games to play, maybe. Or get some videos, or—"

"Leave it to me," Granny said. "Jessie and I will see to everything. I have plans."

Jessie and her mother stared.

"Plans?" asked Rosemary. "What plans?"

Granny smiled mysteriously. "Wait and see," she said, and turned to put the kettle on.

CHAPTER TWO

How Many Toadstools?

Granny wouldn't say another word about the birthday party until she had Rosemary safely tucked up in bed. But at last she came back into the kitchen and sat down again.

Jessie looked at her eagerly. "What plans?" she demanded.

"Well, first, I want you to go and make your bed," Granny said. "You may as well get dressed for the party while you're at it. And I'll wash the dishes and tidy the kitchen."

Jessie's face fell. This wasn't at all the sort of plans she'd had in mind.

But Granny had already started to clear the table, humming one of her strange little songs to herself. Jessie knew it would be useless to argue.

She went off to her bedroom, feeling a bit cross. Of course she knew that her bed had to be made and the room tidied before her friends arrived. And of *course* she had to change her clothes.

But, as Granny had said, three o'clock was hours and hours away. The bedroom could be tidied anytime. She could get changed anytime.

Jessie would much rather have made party plans first.

When Jessie returned to the kitchen, Granny was making fairy cakes. Jessie watched as her grandmother scooped little holes in the tops of the tiny cakes, filled the holes with strawberry jam and cream, and then popped the tops back on.

"Can I sprinkle on the icing sugar?" she asked. She'd helped Granny make fairy cakes before. She loved watching the powdery sugar sprinkling down onto the cakes like snow.

"Not just now," Granny said. "We'll put the icing sugar on just before the party starts. If you put it on too early it can sink into the cakes and disappear."

She looked Jessie up and down. "That's nice. Now you're all ready for the party." She smiled.

Jessie glanced down at her dress. It was pale blue, and usually she liked it. In bright sunshine it looked cool and pretty. But today, because of the rain, it seemed more gray than blue. It looked rather ordinary and dull.

"I wish I had something brighter to wear." She sighed. "This dress is too like the day."

Granny nodded. She understood exactly what Jessie meant. "Gray days do call for bright colors," she said.

She looked at the clock. "Now, I'd like you to do something for me."

"Something for the party?" asked Jessie excitedly. "Something to stop it from being boring?"

"Yes," Granny answered, reaching for more

jam. "I'd like you to go to the pine glade and count the toadstools."

"What?" Jessie exclaimed.

"Count the toadstools," Granny said calmly, without looking up from the fairy cakes. "The red toadstools with white spots, Jessie. You know. Under the pine trees. At the bottom of the garden."

"But . . . but why?"

Granny didn't answer. She frowned with concentration as she topped a tiny cake with cream.

Jessie left the kitchen and went to the back door, wondering what was going on. She looked out at the pouring rain, then down at her party dress and shoes.

"Granny, it's wet out there," she yelled.

"Go barefoot. It's quite warm. Take the red umbrella by the door," Granny called back. "And you don't have to hurry back, Jessie. I'll be fine here. You just enjoy yourself. After all, it *is* your birthday party day."

Jessie pulled off her shoes, grabbed the red umbrella, and went outside.

"Enjoy myself," she grumbled, as she trudged through the rain. "How could I possibly enjoy myself out here?"

She splashed on for a few moments. "And why does Granny need to know how many toadstools there are?" she asked herself. "I'll bet she doesn't. She's just trying to get rid of me for a while, that's all."

She was feeling quite sorry for herself by the time she reached the bottom of the garden. To her right, surrounded by its high hedge, was the still, peaceful place she and Granny called the secret garden. But she couldn't go there today.

She had to go to her left, where the big pine trees clustered right up to the fence between Blue Moon and the Bins' house.

Jessie frowned at the trees. Then she looked beneath them and gasped.

When she'd last visited this part of the garden, seven or eight pretty red-and-white toadstools had dotted the ground between the trees.

But now there were dozens, glowing among the soft brown pine needles. And the pine glade was still, and very quiet, and tingling with magic.

Jessie went in among the trees, breathing in the fresh pine smell. The dark green branches spread overhead like a roof, blotting out the sky and partly sheltering the ground from the rain. She stared around her in wonder.

Granny had said that the red toadstools with white spots came up each year under the pine trees. She had told Jessie that they were just like the toadstools in her grandfather's fairy paintings.

When the first toadstools had appeared a few days ago, after an overnight shower, Jessie had run to tell Granny.

"There'll be more," Granny had said. "And when there are just enough, then . . ."

She'd turned away, smiling mysteriously, and said no more. And in the excitement of counting down the days to her birthday, Jessie had forgotten all about the toadstools under the pine trees, and what her grandmother had said.

Until now.

Jessie's heart thudded. She looked around. Some of the toadstools were big and some were small. They nestled in the thick carpet of pine needles like tiny umbrellas, or little houses with red, white-spotted roofs.

In the middle of the glade stood one toadstool that was bigger than all the rest. The others seemed to surround it. As if it was special.

Jessie blinked and rubbed her eyes. Was she imagining things? Or was there really a tiny doormat in front of the biggest toadstool of all?

She shook her head. It couldn't be! She crept closer, being careful not to crush any of the other toadstools as she stepped between them.

She put her umbrella on the ground and bent down. She peered at the toadstool. Pushed at the tiny doormat with the tip of her finger.

And then she jumped.

She stared.

Lying under the doormat was a tiny golden key.

Jessie picked it up. Her fingers tingled. And suddenly her head was whirling. The pine trees above her were spinning.

The toadstool in front of her was growing. In a moment it was as tall as she was. It was taller!

And then, as her head cleared, Jessie realized that nothing in the pine glade had changed. Except her.

She was tiny. The red umbrella arched like a vast tent behind her. The golden key, which had seemed so very small before, was now heavy in her hand.

The cap of the biggest toadstool reached over her head like a roof. The stem rose up in front of her, tall and wide. And in the stem was a door. A red-painted door.

Just her size.

CHAPTER THREE

The Magic Key

Stuck on the door was a scribbled note: GON FOR HUNNEY. BAK SOON. KUM IN. KEY UNDER MAT.

"What's happened?" whispered Jessie. But, really, she knew the answer.

The golden key was magic. When she'd picked it up, it had made her shrink—to pixie size.

The toadstool was a pixie house, like the toadstools in her grandfather's paintings. And the key she was holding was the key to the door. The pixie who lived in the house must have left it there, expecting friends to call in.

Jessie looked over her shoulder. She could see nothing stirring in the pine glade.

"I'll just have a quick look inside," she said to herself.

She put the key in the lock and turned it. The door swung open to reveal the cutest little room Jessie had ever seen.

Its rounded white walls seemed to glow with soft light. There was a rug of bright green moss on the floor. A hammock made from spiderweb hung in one corner. That must be where the pixie sleeps, Jessie thought.

The room was very tidy. All around the walls hung bunches of red and orange berries, like balloons.

In the middle of the room was a round table covered with bright red mats. On the mats were several brown bowls piled high with cakes, cookies, and round purple-blue fruits that looked like big plums. Right in the center was a large red cake.

It looked as though there was going to be a party. But there was no one there. No one at all.

Jessie just had to have a closer look. She tiptoed through the doorway and into the room.

The first thing she noticed was that just about everything was made from things the pixie had found in the Blue Moon garden.

The table was a piece of smooth bark balanced on a stone. Arranged around it were comfortable-looking couches made from bundles of pine needles tied together with grass.

The mats that covered the table were flower petals. The brown bowls were the little cups that fell from the acorns that grew on Blue Moon's big oak tree. The "plums" were blueberries. And the "cake" in the middle of the table was half a strawberry!

Jessie wandered around, looking at everything. Tucked into the pixie's hammock was a fluffy, pale gray feather. This must be the pixie's blanket.

As she stretched out a finger to touch it, she heard a scuffle in the doorway. She spun around guiltily.

A pixie was standing there, wiping his feet

carefully on the doormat. He had a thin, pointed face and dark, dancing eyes. He wore brightly colored clothes and a striped cap. In his hands he was carrying a gold-wrapped parcel tied up with a piece of grass.

"You're here already, it is!" he exclaimed in a squeaky voice. "And the great red tent—you did bring it, too!" His face creased into a thousand lines as he smiled.

He bounded into the room and handed his parcel to Jessie. "Many happies," he said warmly. Then he looked around. "Old Dingle? Where is he?"

"Is this . . . Old Dingle's place?" asked Jessie. She was finding it hard to take everything in.

"Of course!" said the pixie. "Old Dingle is the oldest. So he has the biggest camp when we come here from the Realm. Of course. Where is he?"

"He . . . he went to get some honey, I think," Jessie stammered. "He left a note on the door."

"Aha! So Old Dingle is not here, it is," exclaimed the pixie in excitement. "But I am here. I, Littlebreeze, am here. So you open mine giftie, now."

Jessica stared at the package she was holding.

The pixie was jumping up and down impatiently. "Yes, yes! Open! You should open mine giftie first, it is," he squeaked, nodding furiously. "Because I gave it to you first."

Jessie swallowed. "This is for me?"

"Of course!" shrieked Littlebreeze. "For your moon-day. Jessie's moon-day. Old Dingle said. We will have a party, it is. For Jessie's moon-day. Old Dingle said."

He glanced at the table and licked his lips. "With treats!" he added.

Amazed, Jessie began opening the package.

"See how I tied it, all mineself?" urged Littlebreeze, dancing around in front of her. "See the nice green tie-up, all new and soft?"

"It's lovely," Jessie agreed, pulling away the piece of grass and laying it on the table.

"And see the real, special wrapping?" Littlebreeze went on. "I have been keeping it very safe, for a special giftie." He patted the package proudly.

Jessie couldn't help smiling. The wrapping

paper was a gold-colored sweet wrapper that someone must have dropped in the garden. It had been smoothed out, and polished till it shone.

"It's beautiful," she said. Carefully, so as not to tear it, she unfolded the paper. She felt quite excited. What wonderful present had Littlebreeze given her? Something strange and magical? Something he'd made himself?

Inside the package was an ordinary gold safety pin.

Jessie stared at it in silence, feeling rather disappointed. A safety pin! What sort of birthday present was that?

In the back of her mind, she heard her grandmother's voice:

See a pin and pick it up
And all the day you'll have good luck.

Granny always said that when she bent to pick up a pin that had fallen to the ground. Then she'd fasten the pin to whatever she was wearing, and leave it there all day. That's why Irena Bins thought

Granny did up her clothes with pins.

Well, this was one pin a pixie had got to first.

Suddenly Jessie realized that Littlebreeze was watching her anxiously, waiting for thanks.

"Oh!" she cried weakly. "Oh, how wonderful. How *useful*. Just what I wanted."

Littlebreeze sighed with satisfaction. "Very old treasure, it is." He nodded. "Very old human treasure."

He touched the pin gently. "I found it, all mineself, four seasons ago, on the grass by the Realm Door," he said. "I have kept it safe, all these many days and nights. And now I give it to you, Jessie, it is. For your moon-day. With many happies."

Jessie looked down at the gold safety pin in her hand, and then at the eager pointed face in front of her. Suddenly she felt ashamed for not understanding how important the pixie's gift was to him.

"Thank you very, very much," she said. "But . . . are you sure you want to give it to me? I mean, it's so precious to you."

Littlebreeze looked surprised. "Of course," he said. "So precious. That is what a giftie should be, it should."

"I'll always keep it safe," said Jessie. She pinned the safety pin carefully to the waist of her dress. It felt quite heavy because she was so small.

Littlebreeze gazed at it. "Look how it shines," he said admiringly. Then he put his head on one side and listened.

"The others are coming!" he exclaimed. He began carefully smoothing and folding the gold paper his present had been wrapped in. Obviously he planned to keep it for use on another "giftie"-giving day.

Jessie ran to the door. And there, behind the arching roof of the red umbrella, she saw dozens of pixies coming toward her, talking and laughing.

Some were walking. Some were running, dodging the raindrops. Some were riding on the backs of little gray lizards. And two, trailing far behind, were perched on the shell of a slow-moving snail.

All of them were brightly dressed, with striped hats and leggings of orange, gold, yellow, purple, green, or red. They all had dark, twinkling eyes and pointed faces.

And all of them were carrying presents.

Littlebreeze squeezed himself into the doorway beside Jessie.

"I was first!" he shouted gleefully to his friends. "Mine giftie was first opening! Old Dingle isn't here, it is!"

"Where is he, then?" squeaked one of the lizard-riding pixies. She stood up on the lizard's back and pretended to peer around. "Where is old slowcoach Dingle-dangle? Fell down a micey hole?"

"I am here, you cheeky Cherry no-good, and I hear you, it is!" roared a deep voice from the back of the crowd.

The lizard-riding pixie clapped her hand over her mouth and sat down quickly.

"Make a way! Honey coming!" roared the deeper voice. "Make a way or be squished!"

The crowd parted, and through the gap drove

a grand old pixie in a wooden cart pulled by two shiny brown beetles.

He drove under the red umbrella and up to the door of the toadstool house. The beetles stopped and pawed the ground.

The old pixie jumped from the cart. Then he whipped off his cap and bowed low to Jessie.

"Many happies, Jessie!" he said. "I am Old Dingle, it is. Welcome! We are honored to share your moon-day."

"Thank you," murmured Jessie. "Thank you very much, for everything. But how did you know? That it was my—um—moon-day? And how did you know I'd be here this morning?"

"A little bird told us!" shrieked the cheeky pixie called Cherry.

Old Dingle frowned fiercely at Cherry, but winked at Jessie. "*Not* a little bird told us," he said. "But a great lady, it is."

"Yes. Queen Jessica herself came and said it to Old Dingle, this morning early," Littlebreeze chipped in. "She said it that you would come. And that you would bring a grand red tent for partying, too. And ever since, we have been making ready, it is."

As Jessie blinked in amazement, Old Dingle raised his arms and faced the eager pixie crowd.

"And now," he roared, "roll down the honey barrel. Start the music. Bring forward the gifties. Let the party begin!"

CHAPTER FOUR

Party Time

There was no way that all the pixies could fit into Old Dingle's house. But that didn't seem to matter to them a bit.

The food was inside, and the music was outside. So pixies who wanted to eat went into the house, and pixies who wanted to dance or sing or play games stayed in the pine glade under the red umbrella.

But before anyone did anything, the "gifties" had to be presented.

While the pixies formed a chattering, excited line, Old Dingle led Jessie to a pine-needle couch beside the party table.

"I gave the first giftie!" exclaimed Littlebreeze, almost bursting with pride.

"Then I give the second, it is," said Old Dingle gravely.

He waited till Jessie had sat down, then bowed again, and presented her with a small package wrapped in pink leaves pinned together with rose thorns.

Jessie pulled out the thorns, and the soft leaves fell away.

"Oh, how beautiful!" She breathed.

Old Dingle had given her a ribbon woven of silvery white silk that glimmered in the light with every color of the rainbow. It was wide and long, but so light that when Jessie held it in her hands it almost floated away.

"You like it, it is," said Old Dingle quietly.

"Oh yes," said Jessie, and meant it with all her heart. "It's so light, and floaty. It looks as though — it looks as though it's made of spiderweb!"

The pixies around her laughed as if she'd made a great joke.

"It *is* made of spidery web, it is." Littlebreeze giggled. "Old Dingle weaves the web like no other pixie. And rain-wet web is the best, the best! It shines. It makes rainbows."

"Put it on!" cried Cherry, jiggling up and down.

Jessie put the shining ribbon around her waist, over the safety pin, and tied it in a bow at the back.

Old Dingle nodded. "Now the princess *looks* like a princess, it is," he said.

Then the other pixies began filing forward, handing over their gifts one by one, telling Jessie their names and the names of all their families, and wishing her "many happies."

There was a carved pinewood comb from Cherry. An acorn bowl of sweet-smelling rosemary leaves from Floss. A berry bracelet from Firethorn. A plaited grass basket from Dawn. Every one of the pixies had brought something special for Jessie's moon-day.

Finally the gift-giving was finished. The last of the long line of pixies had wished Jessie "many happies." And Old Dingle had sent them all away to dance or to eat.

"So you can look at the gifties in peace," he explained to Jessie. "The young ones make a chatter to drive a pixie wild, it is. Loud and fast like twittering birds at sunset."

Jessie laughed, and thanked him. It was true that she was feeling rather dazed after the gift-giving. So many new names and faces. So much talk. So many bright eyes and high voices. She was glad to have a moment to herself to collect her thoughts.

Sitting on the pine-needle couch, she packed her presents into Dawn's basket, ready to take home.

She gazed around her. Some of the pixies were helping themselves to food from the table. Others were just outside the open door, dancing and playing under the shelter of the red umbrella. They were having a wonderful time. And so was Jessie.

"You like the gifties, it is," whispered Littlebreeze, shyly edging up to her. "You like the party we made for you. I can tell by your eyes shining. Will you eat party food now? Sip some honey? Play beetle-hop?"

"I want to do everything!" Jessie laughed, jumping up.

"Food first, Jessie," Cherry called, with her mouth full. "Food is most beautiful."

Littlebreeze led Jessie to the table. The pixies sitting there made room for them, and began passing bowls and plates, begging Jessie to try everything.

Jessie did. It wasn't very long since she'd had breakfast, but she decided that all the excitement must have made her hungry.

The little cakes and cookies heaped in the acorn bowls were delicious! Some, light and soft, smelled of flowers. Some were warm with spices and filled with fruit. Some were chewy with nuts and honey.

There was sweet, lemony drink, too. And blueberries, fresh on Jessie's tongue. The blueberries had come from Granny's garden, but they'd never tasted so good to Jessie before.

Littlebreeze fastened his eyes greedily on the strawberry. A thin, sharp silver knife lay beside it.

"Will you cut your treat soonest, Jessie?" he asked.

"Now! Now!" squeaked Cherry, jumping up and down in her seat.

"Is it time?" Jessie asked.

"When you wish, it is time," rumbled Old Dingle, coming up behind her. "Do you wish?"

Jessie nodded, and he turned to the door.

"Treat-cutting!" he bellowed. "Treat-cutting time! Song-singing time."

There was an excited chattering from outside. The music stopped. Pixies began pouring in to cluster around the table. When the room was full, those who couldn't get in crowded at the door.

"Now, then," said Old Dingle, giving the knife to Jessie.

He raised his hands. All the pixies took deep breaths.

And as Jessie put the knife into the strawberry, Dingle lowered his hands, and the pixies began to sing.

Many happies on your moon-day
Many happies just for you,
May your moon-day be the best day,
May your wishes all come true.

The sound was like a hundred little birds, all singing the one tune. At the end of the song, the pixies began to clap and cheer, shouting Jessie's name, dancing around and beaming.

Jessie nodded and smiled at them. She could feel herself blushing with pleasure.

"It would be helping if I cut the slices, it is," suggested Littlebreeze, eyeing the glistening treat and licking his lips.

"No, let me, me!" shrieked Cherry, pushing toward him.

"*I* will cut the slices," said Old Dingle, taking the knife from Jessie. "As always I do, it is." He frowned severely at the other pixies. "And every slice will be the same size, you greedy ones," he added.

Littlebreeze looked embarrassed, but Cherry giggled. She pulled at Jessie's hand. "Outside now?" she asked. "Play beetle-hop? Berrydropsie? Wobble-walking?"

"I don't know any of those games." Jessie smiled.

"We will teach you," Littlebreeze said, cheering up. "Come on!"

The rain had stopped and a strong wind had sprung up. High above them the tops of the pine trees tossed. But under the red umbrella pixies danced and played in warm, scarlet shelter.

Beetle-hop was a game that involved jumping and sliding over the backs of the big beetles that had pulled Old Dingle's cart.

Jessie was a bit nervous about this at first. The beetles looked very large to her. She thought that they might not like their backs being used for slides.

But she soon realized that there was no danger. The beetles didn't mind the game at all. They could easily have moved away, or shaken the leaping pixies off their backs, but they didn't. They just stood calmly, chewing leaves and looking around them with interest.

Soon Jessie was jumping, sliding, falling into the soft pine needles, and laughing and shouting with everyone else. It was really good fun. She was having a wonderful time.

"Berrydropsie!" squealed Cherry, dragging her away at last. "My best game!"

Berrydropsie was a bit like basketball, except

that there were lots of balls made of bright red berries, and four different baskets made of woven grass.

There were no teams. Everyone played for him- or herself. The idea was to grab as many berries as possible, and throw them into the baskets, which had been fastened to the spokes of the red umbrella.

There didn't seem to be any rules. That didn't matter, though, because as far as Jessie could see, there was no one keeping score either. There were no winners or losers. Everyone was just playing for fun.

Jessie played basketball at school, so she managed to do quite well at berrydropsie.

But wobble-walking was another matter. For that you had to walk as fast as you could across a sort of bouncy net made of woven spiderweb strung between two trees.

The pixies skittered across the net, squealing and wobbling as they went, but staying upright. Jessie kept falling over, then bouncing up so high that her head touched the lowest of the pine branches stretching above her.

Cherry laughed so much that her cap fell off. Jessie laughed, too. And so did Littlebreeze and Old Dingle and all the others. Even the big beetles looked amused. The pine glade was filled with the sound of tiny, twittering voices, the scent of honey and rain-wet pine needles.

And then . . .

"Pixies hide! Humans coming! Humans coming!" squeaked a frightened voice. "Pixies hide!"

In a moment the pixies were scattering everywhere. Piling into Old Dingle's house. Rushing for the other toadstools. Leaping for cover behind the pine trees.

Jessie floundered in the middle of the bouncing spiderweb net, trying to reach the side. Littlebreeze and Cherry held out their arms to her, begging her to hurry.

"I heard something in there, Mum. I did!" boomed a huge unfriendly voice. "I want to see what it is!"

"Irena, don't go over the fence!" screeched another giant voice. "Come back inside!"

Panic gripped Jessie. Her heart beat fast. Irena

Bins from next door was coming into the pine glade! Heavy footsteps thudded on the ground, coming closer.

"Don't worry about me! Run and hide!" Jessie hissed to Littlebreeze and Cherry. She bounced upward, grabbed the branch hanging just above her head, and swung herself up onto it.

"Jessie, do not go too high!" squealed Littlebreeze. Cherry tugged at his arm and together they raced away. Jessie watched as they tumbled into Old Dingle's house and shut the door, pulling the doormat in behind them.

Just in time. Through the tossing trees came Irena, stomping heavily along, her hair blowing in the wind. She was frowning like thunder, kicking at the pine needles in her path.

Jessie clung to the low, swaying branch. Her pale dress fluttered against the dark pine needles. She knew her red hair would be shining and whipping in the wind. Any minute Irena would see her. She was sure of it.

What was she going to do?

CHAPTER FIVE

Up and Away

Jessie began to scramble carefully along her branch toward the trunk of the pine tree. She would have to climb higher, till she was above Irena's head. That would make it harder for Irena to see her.

The rough pine bark was easy to climb. Jessie pulled herself up and up.

"What's this?" she heard Irena say loudly.

She twisted around to see what was happening.

Irena had found the red umbrella. She was bending to pick it up.

"Hey, Mum, those idiots next door have left

an old umbrella here," she shouted. "Will I bring it in?"

"Leave it, Irena," shrieked the other voice. "Let them pick up their own rubbish."

Jessie watched as Irena tossed the umbrella back onto the ground, nearly crushing two of the white-spotted toadstools.

"There are some really horrible-looking toadstools in here, Mum," Irena called. "That crazy Mrs. Belairs probably grows them on purpose."

"Toadstools? Don't you touch them, Irena. They'll be terribly poisonous! Come inside!"

But Irena took no notice. She stamped around the pine glade, staring up into the trees.

"Who'd have a dark, weird place like this in their backyard?" she muttered to herself. "Loonies, that's who."

She walked closer to Jessie's tree.

"I'll bet Jessie left the umbrella here," she yelled to her mother. "She's probably going to make us come here to play during her party. It's the sort of stupid thing she'd think was fun."

Boiling with rage, Jessie climbed higher. The

ground was far below her now, and the wind was stronger. The tree creaked. The branches rocked.

Jessie clung on tightly. With a little pang of fear she remembered Littlebreeze's warning. *Do not go too high,* he'd said. But she told herself she'd had no choice. She couldn't let Irena see her while she was pixie-size.

What am I going to do if she starts to kick at the toadstools? Jessie thought, glancing at Irena.

She looked around for something she could throw. At the end of the branch to which she was clinging she could see a small cluster of pine cones. They would do nicely. She started creeping toward them.

"Irena!" screeched Mrs. Bins. She sounded a long way away. "Will you do as I say and come inside! This wind is shocking!"

"Coming!" roared Irena. "There's nothing here, anyway." She turned and began stomping away across the pine glade.

The wind blew fiercely, gust after gust. Jessie gripped the thin end of her branch as it whipped from side to side.

"Oh, I shouldn't have crawled out here," she whispered to herself.

The wind blew again. The tree bent and swayed. Jessie felt her fingers slipping on the smooth pine needles. She felt herself losing balance . . . slithering from her perch . . .

And then there was another tremendous gust, and Jessie was flying off, off into the air. Like a blown leaf she tumbled helplessly in the wind, over the Blue Moon garden, over the roof of the house.

"Granny! Mum! Littlebreeze! Help!" yelled Jessie at the top of her tiny voice.

But she knew no one could hear her. Her grandmother was in the kitchen, peacefully making party food. Her mother was fast asleep. Her schoolfriends were in their own homes, getting ready to come to her birthday party. The pixies were hiding in their toadstool houses. Her Realm friends were far away in their own world, behind the Door in the secret garden.

No one knew what was happening to her. No one could help her.

The wind blew her on. Over streets and houses. Over the school, the hospital, the park. Below her now were craggy cliffs and bushland.

And still she tumbled through the air, with twigs, leaves, pieces of paper, and other small things that the wind had caught. There was nothing she could do to help herself.

Nothing at all.

At last the gale died down, and Jessie fluttered to the ground.

The fall didn't hurt her. She was so light that she just drifted slowly downward, watching as the bushland rose to meet her. Finally she tumbled onto thick leaves in a small clearing, making hardly any sound.

She sat dazed for a moment, blinking at the prickly bushes and tall trees that surrounded her. Everything looked enormous. She didn't know where she was. All she knew was that she was very far from home.

Pressing her hands together, she tried not to panic. But she was terrified. She was tiny, alone, and helpless. And she had no idea at all what she should do next.

It was still raining a little, but the angry clouds were clearing.

"Rain, rain, go away," she whispered to herself.

She'd said these words only this morning. And that wish had come true, at least. But she wasn't at home to enjoy it. In an hour or two her friends would be arriving for her party. And she wouldn't be there to greet them.

If only she were her normal size! Then she might be able to walk out of here and find a road.

But the pixies and the magic key were in the pine glade at Blue Moon. And she was here, in the middle of nowhere.

Jessie fell back on the ground and covered her face. Of all the magical adventures she'd had since she'd discovered the Realm, this was the most terrifying. Because this time she was all alone.

"All will be well," she seemed to hear her grandmother say.

Not this time, she thought. *This time I'll never get home.* Hot tears began to roll down her cheeks.

There was a thumping sound high above her. A shower of twigs and leaves pattered onto her face and shoulders.

Jessie's eyes flew open in terror. Through her tears she could see a monstrous, brightly colored shape looming over her.

"What's up with you?" croaked a harsh voice.

Jessie screamed.

Round black eyes peered down at her. A huge, curved beak opened. "Nothing wrong with your voice, anyway," the creature said.

Jessie rubbed her tears away and stared. Then she saw what the brightly colored monster was. It was a red, green, and yellow parrot, bobbing up and down on a twig beside her.

It put its head on one side. "Saw you fall out of the sky," it croaked. "Came down to have a look. You don't see fairies around here too often. Get wet wings, did you?"

"I'm . . . not a fairy," said Jessie. "I'm a human."

The parrot shrieked with laughter. The sound was deafening. Jessie covered her ears and shut her eyes.

"Oh, sorry," said the parrot. "Forgot myself for a minute." It leaned over and lowered its voice.

"Listen, small stuff, you must have bumped your head when you fell. You're all confused. You're not a human. You wouldn't be as big as a human's finger. You're a pipsqueak, girl. You're itsy-bitsy. You're teeny-weeny. And if you aren't a fairy, what are you?"

Jessie sat up. "I *am* a human," she said. "I am a human who was made small by pixies. And—"

The parrot squawked. "Pixies!" it screeched. "Pixies! Oh, well, that explains it. I should have known. Like my old dad used to say, where pixies go, trouble follows."

"That's not fair," Jessie protested. "We were just having a party, and someone came, and everyone had to hide, and I got blown away by the wind. It wasn't—"

"Oh, I know." The parrot sniffed. "It wasn't the pixies' fault. It never is, girl. Things just . . . happen when they're around, that's all. I've seen it, time and again."

It put its head on one side and stared at Jessie.

"The point is," it said, "here you are, pixie-size and lost. What are you going to do about it?"

Jessie opened her mouth and closed it again.

"Don't know, do you?" squawked the parrot. "Don't have the faintest clue."

"Couldn't you help me?" begged Jessie. "I mean, couldn't you help me get home?"

CHAPTER SIX

The End of the Rainbow

"Where's home?" asked the parrot.

Jessie swallowed. "I don't know," she admitted. "I mean, I know my address, but I don't suppose—"

"No. Addresses don't mean anything to me, girl," said the parrot. "Places are what I know."

"Well, I live in a town with a school, and a park and a hospital. And my house is big and old with a lovely garden and a hedge and a pine glade and—"

The parrot fluffed up its feathers and settled itself more comfortably on its twig. "This isn't helping, girl," it said severely. "I see dozens of towns like that, thousands of houses like that, in a week."

Suddenly Jessie had a wonderful idea. She jumped to her feet. "A phone!" she exclaimed. "Could you take me out of here and get me to a phone? Then I could ring my grandmother, and she could come and get me."

The parrot cocked its head. "Good thinking!" it said admiringly. "All right! You climb up here and— What's the matter?"

For Jessie's face had fallen. She looked as though she was about to cry again.

"I've just realized, I can't ring up," she said. "I'm too little to lift the receiver. My hands are too small to dial the numbers. And I think my voice is too tiny to be heard through a phone anyway."

"Hm." The parrot scratched thoughtfully under one wing.

"This is so awful!" Jessie wailed. "I can't get back to my normal size unless I get home! And I can't get home because I'm not my normal size!"

She thumped her hands together in frustration, and the charm bracelet on her wrist jingled softly. She looked down at it.

"If my Realm friends were here—Maybelle, or Patrice, or even Giff, I'm sure they'd know what to do," she murmured. "They'd know how to get me back home. Or they could get me into the Realm, through a Door."

"What's this you're talking about?" asked the parrot curiously.

"The Realm." Jessie sighed. "A magic place I know. The pixies come from there. And I have other friends there, too. They could help me. They could change me back to my normal size. They could get me home. If only I could find a Door."

The parrot was listening carefully. "There are lots of Doors to this Realm place, are there?" it asked.

Jessie nodded. "Yes. At least, that's what they say. But I only know one. And it's—"

"Back at your home, I know!" the parrot finished for her. "You know, we're going round in circles, girl."

Jessie nodded sadly.

The parrot broke off a seed pod and nibbled at it thoughtfully. "Don't let it get you down," it mumbled at last. "Things are tough, but they could be worse."

"How?"

"It could still be raining," said the parrot. "Look on the bright side. The wind blew you away. But it blew the clouds away as well. The sun's shining. And look up there. Now, that's a pretty sight."

It stretched its bright wings. "I do like a nice bit of color," it added. "Go on, girl, have a look! Cheer yourself up."

To be polite, Jessie looked up. For a moment she just stared. Then her heart leaped into her throat.

Arching overhead was a perfect rainbow.

"Nice, isn't it?" remarked the parrot. "Looks like it ends just over the hill."

Jessie was remembering. "There's more than just a pot of gold at the end of the rainbow, you know," Granny had said that morning. "There's always a Door to the Realm, too. If you find the rainbow's end you have to choose. The gold, or a visit to the Realm."

"Oh!" cried Jessie. "Oh! Oh, parrot, quickly. The rainbow! The rainbow!"

"What about it?"

"I need to get to the end of the rainbow," Jessie gabbled, seizing a twig and hoisting herself up into the bush. "Will you take me there?"

"How can you think about gold at a time like this?" snapped the parrot. "You're in trouble, girl. You're lost and shrunk to practically nothing, don't you remember?"

"It's not the gold," Jessie puffed, struggling up the prickly bush. "It's a way home! Will you take me there? Will you? Please?"

"We'll have to hurry," the parrot said, eyeing the rainbow doubtfully. Jessie looked up and to her horror saw that the bright colors were already fading.

She made a final effort, swung herself up to the parrot's twig and climbed on its back. Its feathers felt soft and slippery.

"All right, then," the parrot said. "We'll have a go. Can't promise anything, but I'll see what I can do. Hold tight!"

With a screech that nearly deafened Jessie it spread its wings and launched itself into the air.

Jessie crouched low, desperately trying to stop herself from falling. The breeze whistled past her ears. Up, up the parrot flew, its wings beating steadily. It soared over the tops of the trees and climbed higher.

Now the misty blue sky was all around them. And arching overhead was the rainbow, glowing red and purple, green, orange, yellow . . .

Over the parrot's shoulder Jessie could see a low hill. The rainbow seemed to end just on the other side.

But did it really? Jessie had chased rainbows before, and never once had she found the place where one touched the earth. Always it had been just a little farther away than she'd thought. And no matter how fast she'd run, she'd never quite reached it before the rainbow's colors faded away.

But she had never chased a rainbow from the air. She had never had such a good, clear view of the rainbow's end.

Perhaps this time it would be different.

As the parrot winged its way over the hill, Jessie saw something that made her heart leap with hope. The arching color dipped onto the earth just ahead of them, flooding a small group of trees with pink and golden light.

"There!" she screamed in excitement. "There! In that little cluster of trees. Near the big rock. There's the rainbow's end!"

"We haven't got much time, girl," puffed the parrot. "Be ready, now. Ready to jump off and go for it."

The rainbow's colors were growing lighter and lighter with every second. It was as if they were dissolving into the blue of the sky, like sugar crystals disappearing in water. Soon they would be gone, and Jessie's chance to find the Door to the Realm would be gone, too.

"Oh, hurry, hurry!" she pleaded.

The parrot began zooming toward the cluster of trees. Jessie shut her eyes. She was so afraid that the rainbow would disappear while she watched.

"Nearly there," the parrot screeched. "Get ready!"

Jessie opened her eyes. Yes! The rainbow colors were faint, but they were there. The grove of trees glimmered with pale gold light. There was still a chance.

With a rush of fluttering wings the parrot landed on the topmost branch of the tallest of the trees. All around them colored lights danced and swirled. Jessie caught her breath. It was so beautiful! So . . .

"Hurry!" squawked the parrot, jiggling on the branch. "It's going! Quickly! Jump!"

And Jessie jumped. Jumped right into the swirling light, and drifted down, down, down to the earth.

"Gold, or the Realm . . . the Realm . . . the Realm?" It was a voice like an echoing silvery bell.

Jessie gasped. For a moment she couldn't speak.

"You must answer . . . answer," called the voice softly. "The colors are fading from the sky. We must go . . . go. Gold, or the Realm?"

"The Realm!" Jessie burst out.

"So be it!" called the silvery voice. "Open . . . Open . . . Open!"

Jessie heard the rushing sound of the opening Door, and felt the familiar cool wind on her face and in her hair. There was an explosion of color. Then she felt herself tumbling and spinning through the Door.

Into the Realm.

CHAPTER SEVEN

The Rainbow Fairies

Colors swirled around Jessie like thick, glittering mist. Waves of palest pink, shining gold, clear green, sky blue, soft purple . . .

"Welcome to the Realm . . . the Realm." The silvery, echoing voice seemed to come from all around her. "Who are you? Who are you?"

"I am Jessie," Jessie said, blinking. She couldn't see who was speaking. She held up her hands, trying to brush the color mists aside.

Soft laughter rose and fell around her. Then Jessie felt cool fingers taking her hands and leading her forward.

She couldn't see where she was going, or who was guiding her. The color mists seemed to fill her eyes and ears, making her dizzy.

"We are nearly there, now . . . now . . . now," sang the silvery voice. "Soon . . . soon . . . soon."

Jessie peered into the mists in front of her. Was it her imagination, or were they clearing a little?

She stumbled forward a few more steps, and knew that she was right. Now the swirling colors were paler, and she could see shapes around and ahead of her. Moving, fluttering, gliding shapes. Lots of them.

"Who are you?" she asked.

"We are the rainbow fairies . . . rainbow fairies . . . rainbow fairies."

Again the silvery sound came from all around her. And at last Jessie realized that all this time she had been listening not to just one voice, but to many. The rainbow fairies had been speaking together, in a chorus.

The cool fingers tugged at her hands, urging her to move forward more quickly.

"Come, Jessie . . . Jessie . . . Jessie."

In front of her Jessie could now see the shapes of trees. She could see lots more movement, too. Gradually the light was changing. The blues and greens had faded away, and she was seeing everything through a golden haze, shot with pink.

And then she had stepped out of the color mists, and was standing on soft green grass, breathing the familiar sweet air of the Realm. But this was not like any part of the Realm she'd seen before. Shining crystals lay heaped on the grass, flashing with rainbow colors in the sun. Everything was vividly bright and clear.

"Jessie! Jessie!"

The bell-like voices echoed in her ears.

Slim figures dressed in every color of the rainbow surrounded her—fairies with smooth golden skin, golden hair, and deep green eyes. Their shining wings were transparent, like a dragonfly's wings, and changed color as they moved. Around their necks they wore strings of the same bright crystals that lay around them in piles.

The fairies stared at Jessie with startled eyes. She realized that they were surprised to see that she was so tiny.

"I—I am a human child," she stammered. "I have been made small by magic."

The fairies went on staring at her, then moved together and bent their heads as they murmured to one another.

The crystals and the changing colors of the fairies' wings were dazzling. Jessie's eyes started to water and she rubbed at them.

"You are free to wander . . . wander in the Realm," said the rainbow fairies, after a moment. "Return to us when you wish to go back through the Door. We will be there . . . there . . . there."

They pointed.

Jessie turned to look behind her, where the color mists swirled, thick and full of light. Flickering through the mists were the shapes of other fairies, bending and reaching for something in the mists.

As she watched, fairies moved out of the mists,

carrying handfuls of flashing crystals. They placed them carefully on the crystal heaps and slipped back into the mists again.

"What are they doing?" she asked.

"They are gathering the color . . . the color," sang the rainbow fairies. "They are working. There is much to do . . . do . . . do. Soon we must join them. But you can wander in the Realm . . . the Realm as you wish . . . wish . . . wish. No harm will come to you here . . . here . . ."

Jessie rubbed her hands over her eyes again. The flashing light, the brightness of the color, and the echoing voices were making it hard for her to think.

"Could I . . . could you take me to Queen Helena's palace?" she asked at last.

The rainbow fairies stared at her, and then at one another. Their deep green eyes were like still water. For once, they couldn't seem to decide what to say.

"It's all right. I know Queen Helena," Jessie said quickly. "Really I do. And anyway, I won't trouble her. I just need to get to a Door that's near the palace. It's a Door that will take me home."

"Queen Helena . . . Door . . . home . . ." the rainbow fairies whispered. They went on staring at Jessie. She wasn't sure if they believed her or not.

"Oh, *please* take me to the palace!" Jessie burst out. "Or at least show me the way."

"We cannot leave here now . . . now," chimed the fairies. "The rainbow colors must be gathered and trapped in the crystals while they are fresh and new . . . new . . . new."

They began drifting back toward the mists.

"But if I don't get home soon, and get back to my normal size, I'll miss my own birthday party," Jessie wailed after them. "And my mother will be so worried about me. I need your help. I'm lost!"

The rainbow fairies turned. Jessie realized that something she had said had at last got through to them.

"Lost?" said one. It was the first time Jessie had heard any of the fairies speak alone.

"Yes!" Jessie exclaimed. "I'm lost. I need your help."

The fairy who had spoken held out her golden hand. Her dragonfly wings slowly opened and shut behind her, fanning the color mists into swirls. Jessie saw that her green eyes were sad.

"I am Emerald," she said. "Once, long ago, I was lost."

"Well, you know how it feels, then," said Jessie.

Emerald bowed her head. "It feels gray," she murmured. "Lonely gray, and sad dark blue and purple. And then flashes of bright red fear come. You can feel them. Here." She put her hand to her chest.

Jessie felt a lump in her throat. "Yes," she said. "That's just how it feels."

Emerald turned and spoke to the other fairies.

Jessie clasped her hands. Were they going to help her?

Two of the fairies slipped away from the group and drifted into the color mists. Emerald turned back to Jessie.

"We cannot leave this place just now," she said. "But others can guide you to the palace. They are coming soon, to take away some color crystals. We will ask them to help you. My sisters have gone to watch for them."

Jessie felt a huge wave of relief wash over her. "Thank you," she said.

"We must help you if you are lost . . . lost," all the rainbow fairies said together. "It is gray to be lost."

"How were you lost, Jessie?" Emerald asked.

"I was blown away from my garden by a big wind," said Jessie.

Emerald nodded. "When I was lost, it started in a human garden also," she said. "It was four seasons ago, when I was very new. I was watching baby rainbows in the water that was sprinkling on the flowers. I would not leave with my friends. I liked it in the garden."

"We remember . . . remember . . ." the fairies around her chorused.

"As the sun dipped lower in the sky some pixies came. They were camping nearby. They were yellow and orange, green and red, laughing and singing," said Emerald. "I had never met pixies before. They taught me games. We played. I did not see that time had passed. Then, suddenly the sun went down."

"The sun went down . . . down . . . down . . ." echoed the other fairies sadly.

"The pixies ran off to their camp. I was alone." Emerald sighed. "The sprinkling water still wet the flowers, but the baby rainbows had gone. The earth colors changed and went dim. I could not see. I could hear the pixies laughing far away, but I could not find them."

She shivered. "I could not find the Door either. And it was cold. So cold. I knew that if I could not find the Door very soon, I would die."

Her golden wings grew pale and her wings glimmered silver, as she remembered. The other fairies clustered around her, stroking her hair.

"What happened?" Jessie asked. "Who saved you?"

In Emerald's green eyes a spark began to glow. "A great lady," she said. "A great lady came to the garden. As tall as one of the Folk, she was. A big cat padded at her side. It was monstrous, with eyes that gleamed in the darkness.

"I was deathly afraid—stabbing scarlet fear. I hid, but still the lady saw me. She bent down and smiled, and spoke to me.

"'Do not fear, little fairy,' she said, so gently. 'Do not cry. I will take you back through the Door. All will be well.'"

"All will be well," echoed the other rainbow fairies.

Jessie's heart leaped. She knew those words. She knew someone who said them all the time.

CHAPTER EIGHT

Emerald's Treasure

"What was this garden like?" Jessie asked. "This garden where you were lost?"

"It was a sweet, still garden," said Emerald, "with a high hedge all around. Outside the hedge, tall trees rustled in the wind, and there was a big human house with lighted windows."

She looked at Jessie. "Do you know such a place?"

"I think I might," said Jessie. "But, please, go on with your story."

"The lady was kind, but I could not stop my tears," Emerald continued. "I shivered and cried, and would not look at her."

"'I cannot take you back through the Door unless you are strong in your heart, little fairy,' she said. 'You must try your best to trust me, and be calm.'

"But still I trembled and wept. The lady looked down at the monster cat, purring beside her. 'Whatever am I going to do with this small one?' she asked it.

"The cat made a sound. The lady nodded. 'Perfect,' she said. She took something from her dress and gave it to me. It was a treasure that glittered, even in the gloom. Curiously shaped, and smooth to touch.

"'Look at this pretty thing,' she said. 'See how it shines?'

"I looked at the treasure, shining like the gold at the rainbow's end, and she told me it was magic. I was so amazed and filled with wonder that my tears stopped, and I began to smile.

"'Wonderful!' cried the lady. 'Now you are ready to go home.' She took me in her hand. She cried, 'Open,' in the great voice of the Folk. And the Door opened wide, and she took me through. To the Realm, and safety."

"Safety . . ." sang the fairies.

Emerald looked down. "I was so excited," she whispered. "Bright yellow joy filled my heart. I darted off at once to the rainbow's end, to find my friends. I left the lady standing on the road by the Door, alone."

Her voice dropped to a sigh. "Just once I looked back. She smiled and waved to me. Of course she thought that I would return to her garden one day soon. To thank her, and return her treasure."

"And didn't you?" asked Jessie.

Emerald bent her head. Her wings drooped. "I could not," she said. "To my shame, I could not."

"Why?"

"Somehow I had dropped the treasure she had let me hold to calm my fear," whispered Emerald. "In the first excitement of reaching the Realm I forgot all about it. Then, later, I remembered. I remembered it falling from my hand as the lady took me through the Door."

Tears welled up in her beautiful green eyes. "I was sure it had fallen to the ground in the sweet garden. But the next day, at sunrise, when my friends and I crept back to try to find it, it was gone."

She buried her face in her hands. "I had lost the great lady's treasure. I knew she would never forgive me."

"You were very new then . . . very new," chimed the other fairies, fluttering around her.

Emerald shook her head. "There is no excuse. I did not thank the lady. And now I never can. I dropped her treasure. It is lost. Four seasons have gone by, and still I am filled with shame. I could not face the lady now."

Jessie took a deep breath. "Do you know who the lady was?" she asked.

Emerald's lips trembled. "This is the worst part of all. Since that day I have learned more about the garden. I have come to believe that the lady was Jessica, the Realm's true Queen. I am sure it was she. I still see her face in my dreams."

Tears rolled down her cheeks. "I have stolen

treasure from our Queen. Never again can I return to that beautiful garden. And none of my sisters can go back either."

"None of us can go back . . . back . . ." murmured the other fairies.

Jessie held out her hand.

"Emerald, please don't cry," she said. "There's no need for you to be sad anymore. Or to stay away from the secret garden. Queen Jessica loves to have you there. She told me herself."

"You *know* the true Queen?" stammered Emerald.

"Queen Jessica is my grandmother," said Jessie quietly. "My mother and I live with her, in that big house with the lighted windows you told me about."

Emerald and all the other rainbow fairies gasped and stepped back.

"It's all right," cried Jessie. "Don't you see? My grandmother saved you when you were lost, Emerald. Now you have saved me. It's wonderful!"

Emerald's tearful face lit up. Then a shadow crossed it again. "The treasure . . ." she began.

"Granny—Queen Jessica—won't mind about that," said Jessie firmly. "She doesn't care about *things*. Only about people. She's told me, often. I'll explain everything to her. She'll understand. She always understands."

"It was a very great and fine treasure," Emerald said doubtfully. "Gold like the rainbow's end. And magic, too."

Jessie frowned. Granny hadn't said anything about losing something so valuable. What could it be?

"Are you *sure* it was magic?" she asked.

"Oh yes," Emerald said. "It clung to her dress without a cord or thread to hold it."

"Without a cord or thread . . . thread," echoed her friends, their green eyes wide.

"And, besides, when the lady gave the treasure to me she said, "Now *you* can have good luck for a while, little fairy." She laughed as she said it. But I knew she meant that the treasure was magic. It brought good fortune."

Good luck? Jessie clapped her hand to her waist. Was it possible?

See a pin and pick it up
And all the day you'll have good luck.

How many times had she heard Granny say those words? How many times had she seen Granny fasten a pin to her dress and wear it around all day?

And what had Littlebreeze said as he proudly watched her unwrap his "giftie"?

"Very old treasure," he had said. "Very old human treasure. I found it, all mineself, four seasons ago, on the grass by the Realm Door."

Slowly Jessie pulled aside Old Dingle's spider-web sash to show Emerald the safety pin fastened to the waist of her dress.

Emerald screamed, and pointed with a trembling finger. "The treasure!" she cried. "The lady's treasure. It's found!"

All the other fairies began fluttering and leaping around Jessie. Attracted by the noise, dozens of others began gliding from the color mists, their hands filled with flashing crystals.

There was so much noise and excitement that

no one paid any attention to the three shadows bumbling around in the mists.

No one heard the shouting and snorting as someone stamped crossly through the clouds of color. No one heard the high wailing as someone else called out that he was dizzy. No one heard a third voice cheerfully telling them both to stop fussing.

It wasn't until the three figures appeared at the edge of the mists that Jessie saw them. And then she shouted with joy, unable to believe her eyes.

"Maybelle, Giff, Patrice! You're here!"

CHAPTER NINE

old friends

Jessie ran forward, her arms outstretched. But when the three figures stumbled out of the color mists, she stopped and stared.

She'd been sure that these were her friends from the Realm. Yet . . . suddenly she wasn't sure at all. They didn't show any sign of recognizing her. And they looked—different.

The person she'd thought was Patrice the palace housekeeper *looked* like Patrice. But she was younger than the Patrice Jessie knew. Her round cheeks were pinker, and her clothes were brilliantly colored.

The person she'd thought was Giff the elf had bright, sparkling eyes. The tips of his pointed ears were red. His clothes were the light, vivid green of new leaves.

And Maybelle—of *course* this wasn't Maybelle. Maybelle was white. This was another miniature horse altogether, a horse whose coat shimmered pink, sky blue, soft mauve.

Jessie hesitated as the three strangers approached the rainbow fairies and the heaps of flashing crystals.

"What do you mean by rushing off and leaving us in that fog?" snapped the miniature horse, shaking her mane crossly at the fairies.

"Oh dear, oh dear!" wailed the elf, holding his head. "I'm all dizzy. I can't think!"

"You never *do* think very well, dearie," said the person Jessie had thought was Patrice. "So don't try. Just stand still and keep out of trouble."

The miniature horse snorted. And that snort changed Jessie's mind all over again. No one else could snort like that.

"Maybelle!" she squeaked.

The miniature horse turned her head. "Who called my name?" she asked sharply.

The rainbow fairies murmured to one another and fluttered their wings nervously.

"It's me! Me!" Jessie screamed, jumping up and down. "Maybelle! Patrice! Giff! It's me, Jessie!"

The three looked around in puzzlement. They couldn't see her.

Jessie waved frantically. "Over here!" she shouted.

All of a sudden the elf noticed her. His face broke into an enormous grin. "Jessie!" he exclaimed.

"What do you mean, 'Jessie,'" huffed the miniature horse. "You foolish elf! Jessie's not here."

"I am, I am!" cried Jessie, jumping up and down.

Patrice threw up her hands in shock. "Jessie! It *is* you!" She hurried to Jessie's side and stood towering over her. "Oh, my dear! We didn't see you. We didn't notice you. You're so . . . so . . ."

"So little!" said Maybelle, trotting over to join

them. “What in the Realm have you been doing to yourself?”

Patrice clasped her hands. “I know!” she exclaimed. “I know! It’s pixies, isn’t it! You’ve been playing with pixies!”

“Yes,” Jessie admitted in a small voice. “They’re camping in the Blue Moon garden, you see. In toadstools.”

“Oh dear, oh dear,” moaned Giff. “Poor you.” He stretched out a finger and stroked Jessie’s head.

“But how did you get *here*?” Patrice demanded. “Still small, and all? Why didn’t they get you back to normal before you left them?”

“Um . . . it’s a long story,” said Jessie. “It wasn’t their fault. I . . . ran into a bit of trouble.”

“I thought as much,” snorted Maybelle. “Pixies! Where they go, trouble follows. Like night follows day.”

“Everything ended up all right,” Jessie protested. “Didn’t it?”

“We’ll see,” said Maybelle darkly.

Emerald drifted toward them. Jessie saw that

her deep green eyes were no longer sad. Now they were shining with happiness. Well, *that's* something that's turned out well, anyway, she thought, and felt better.

Emerald bowed to Patrice and Maybelle.

"We have been awaiting your visit. Could you lead our dear friend Jessie to the palace?" she asked.

"The palace . . . the palace . . ." echoed the other rainbow fairies, clustering close behind her.

"She's *our* friend, too, you know!" exclaimed Giff crossly.

"We will certainly take her to the palace," said Patrice to Emerald. "Queen Helena will have to know about this."

She shook her head. "I never saw anything like it. Our true Queen's granddaughter, pixie-size. What a disgrace!"

"Let's go," said Maybelle. She pawed the ground impatiently. As she did, she looked in disgust at her leg, shining mauve and pink.

"Look at that!" she huffed. "What sort of color is that for a horse!"

"The colors will fade . . . fade . . ." chimed the silvery voices of the rainbow fairies. "By sunrise tomorrow . . . tomorrow."

"I *know* that," said Maybelle. "But I don't like it all the same."

"*I* like it," said Patrice. "This place does me the world of good. Makes me feel like a girl again."

"You look so much younger, Patrice," said Jessie. "I didn't recognize you at first."

Patrice bent and picked her up. "*You* didn't recognize *me*!" She laughed. "Well, I can tell you, if I look different, you look even *more* different, my girl."

She turned to Giff. "Go and get the color crystals, Giff," she ordered. "And make sure they give you plenty of blues. Queen Helena particularly asked for blue."

Giff nodded and scurried away. Three of the rainbow fairies flew after him.

Jessie smiled down at Emerald. "Thank you for everything," she called softly. "I hope—I hope I might see you again soon. In the secret garden.

There's no reason for you to stay away now, is there?"

She patted her waist where the safety pin lay hidden.

Emerald spread her wings and fluttered into the air. She hovered beside Patrice's hand and looked into Jessie's eyes. The heaps of crystals flashed behind her. Her wings shone with every color of the rainbow.

"We will all come to see you, Jessie," she said, holding out her arms. "And to see our true Queen, too. As you say, there is no reason for us to stay away . . . now."

"I've got them," Giff bellowed, stumbling back from between the piles of crystals, carrying a big sack. "Can we go now? Patrice? Maybelle?"

Patrice nodded briskly to Emerald. "The Queen thanks you for your good work," she said.

Emerald and the other fairies bowed low.

"Let's get out of here," huffed Maybelle. "Come on!"

"I will lead you through the mists," said

Emerald. "Please follow."

She moved into the waves of color. Maybelle and Giff went after her. Patrice, holding Jessie carefully in her hand, stayed close behind.

The color mists closed in around them. Blue and green, pink and purple, orange and gold . . .

"This way, this way," called Emerald, darting to and fro in front of them so they could not lose sight of her.

"I hate this," grumbled Maybelle, tossing her head. "Now I'll go even pinker. You and Giff can come on your own next time, Patrice."

"I don't like it either," Giff moaned. "All these different colors make me feel funny."

"Stop complaining, you two," said Patrice. "Look on the bright side. Because you came with me this time you met up with Jessie. Think how cross you'd have been if you'd missed her."

"This way," sang Emerald. "Nearly there . . . nearly there . . ."

The color clouds began to thin, and soon Emerald was leading Jessie and her friends out into pure air and light again.

Ahead of them stretched a broad field of flowers, ringed by thick forest. Dozens of narrow paths threaded through the field, twisting and turning before they disappeared among the trees.

"I'm glad I'm not trying to find my way alone," Jessie said to Patrice.

"You'd never have done it, dearie," Patrice replied comfortably.

"Travel well," said Emerald. "I must go back to my sisters now. There is much to do."

She flew back to the edge of the color mists and hovered there, surrounded by streaks of gold and pink.

"Goodbye!" called Jessie. "Goodbye, Emerald."

The fairy waved her hand. Then she turned and darted back into the mists.

"Goodbye, Jessie!" they heard her sing. "Goodbye." Her voice seemed to echo as hundreds of other bell-like voices chimed in.

"Goodbye, Jessie . . . Jessie," the rainbow fairies called. "Goodbye . . . goodbye . . . goodbye."

CHAPTER TEN

Happy Endings

It took a very long time for them to walk to the palace, and on the way Jessie told her friends the story of her adventures.

She didn't tell them about Emerald and Granny, of course. That was the rainbow fairies' secret, and something they had worried about very much. They wouldn't like other people knowing about it.

"So . . . I have to get back to the pine glade," Jessie finished. "Then I can ask the pixies to change me back to my normal size."

"I wouldn't depend on *them,*" Maybelle said

scornfully. "They could have moved on by now. Or be off playing some game. Getting some other poor creature into trouble."

"Maybelle, I *told* you! What happened to me wasn't their fault!" cried Jessie. "I don't know why everyone is so down on pixies. I think they're lovely. Lovely, and clever, and so happy! They're so good at making do with what they have. So . . . full of fun!"

"Oh yes, they're all that." Maybelle sniffed. "And I don't say they don't mean well. It's just . . . You ask Giff what happened when he went off with the pixies the spring before last."

Giff's red-tipped ears drooped. "We played leafboats and I fell in the river," he confessed. "The pixies said it would be a good idea for me to take off my clothes to dry them. So I did. I hung them on a bush. Then a unicorn ate them. Jacket, shirt, trousers—even my hat."

Jessie smothered a giggle. "Oh, that's awful, Giff." She choked.

"Go on, laugh," gloomed Giff. "Everyone else did, when I got home."

Patrice was quite red in the face. Her shoulders shook, jiggling Jessie up and down. "We couldn't help it. You looked so *funny* dressed up in those flower petals the pixies gave you," she hooted.

Maybelle rolled her eyes. "Like a dear little flower fairy, weren't you, Giff!" she said.

"Oh, don't tease him!" pleaded Jessie. "After all, I've made much more of a mess of things. My birthday party will be starting at three o'clock, and here I am, still pixie-size and in the Realm."

"We'll make it," said Maybelle. She broke into a trot. Giff and Patrice started to jog. Jessie bounced on Patrice's shoulder, holding on to her hair.

A few minutes later they burst into the palace, through the great golden doors at the front entrance. The guards stood back as soon as they saw Patrice.

"We must see Queen Helena at once!" she said crisply.

The guards saluted. "In the throne room, Ma'am," said one. He glanced at Jessie, perched on Patrice's shoulder, and his eyebrows rose.

"Come along Giff, Maybelle," said Patrice,

ignoring him. "We have to hurry. It's nearly three o'clock."

It took only a few moments to explain things to Queen Helena. She wasn't cross, as Patrice had been. She just laughed.

"Where pixies go, trouble follows," she said, shaking back her long golden red hair, so like Jessie's own. "But they're such fun, aren't they, Jessie?"

Jessie laughed, too, and nodded.

"Your grandmother loves them so much," Queen Helena went on. "She always used to say that anyone who felt grouchy, anyone who had forgotten how to be glad just to be alive, should spend some time with the pixies."

"I think that's why she sent me to see them," Jessie admitted. "She probably thought the best way to make sure my party went well was to make sure *I* was happy first."

"Maybe." Queen Helena's green eyes twinkled. "Though I don't suppose she planned for you to have *such* an exciting time."

She asked Patrice to put Jessie down on the floor. She stretched out her hand and closed her eyes. Then she hesitated.

"Are you wearing anything that's pixie-made, Jessie?" she asked. "If so, take it off."

Jessie quickly pulled Old Dingle's spider-silk ribbon from around her waist. Of course! It wouldn't grow with her. It was lucky Queen Helena had thought of it. It would have been a shame if it had ripped and torn.

Queen Helena began whispering some strange words.

Jessie felt a tingle spread from her toes to the top of her head. And then, with a dizzying rush, she felt herself growing, hurtling toward the ceiling.

It was like a crazy roller-coaster ride that just seemed to go on and on.

Jessie screwed her eyes shut. "Oh, I'm getting too big!" she screamed.

But when the ground under her feet was still again, and her head had stopped spinning, she opened her eyes. And then she could see that she wasn't too big at all. She was just back to normal.

She looked in amazement at the delicate ribbon that hung from her fingers. She had worn that as a sash.

"Was I *that* tiny?" she exclaimed.

"You certainly were," said Patrice. "But you look much better now. It's lucky you're already dressed for the party, anyway. That will save some time."

Jessie stared down at her dress. It was the first time she'd really looked at herself since she was blown away from the pine glade.

She blinked and shook her head. She still felt a bit dizzy after having grown so fast.

"We should get Jessie back home now," Maybelle told Queen Helena. "Her guests will be arriving at Blue Moon any minute. I'll go with her. No one will see me if I'm quick. I suppose *someone* had better tell those pixies what became of her."

Jessie nodded. She was still looking at her dress. And suddenly she couldn't stop smiling.

"I hope your party today is the best ever, Jessie," beamed Giff.

"Oh, it will be, Giff." Queen Helena laughed. "Can't you see that already?'

It *was* a wonderful party. Everyone said so. In fact, a lot of Jessie's friends said it was the best birthday party they'd ever been to. But no one quite knew why.

Except Jessie. The party had been happy because *she* was happy. Not nervous, or worried, or shy. Just happy, and full of jokes and fun, like the pixies. And that made all her friends feel comfortable and happy, too.

All except Irena Bins, of course. She just sulked and frowned and hung around with her nose in the air.

"I thought you said you weren't getting a new dress for the party," she'd said to Jessie crossly, when she arrived.

"I didn't," Jessie answered. She lifted a fold of her old dress—not plain pale gray-blue any longer, but sparkling and shimmering with every color of the rainbow.

Irena sniffed disbelievingly. "Well, where did you get that hair ribbon?" she demanded. "I've never seen one like that before. The way it floats and shines . . ."

"Like spiderwebs after the rain," said Sal, touching the ribbon.

"Don't be stupid." Irena frowned. And stumped off to stand all by herself.

Jessie, Rosemary, and Granny waved the last guest goodbye and shut the door.

"What a lovely party that was." Rosemary sighed. "Oh, I'm glad everything went so well."

She went off to the kitchen to make a pot of tea.

"It was a wonderful idea to dye Jessie's old dress like that, Mum," she called back over her shoulder. "It looks beautiful. I don't know how you did it."

Granny raised her eyebrows at Jessie. "I'm not quite sure either. I've been waiting till the party was over so I could talk to Jessie about it," she called back. "But if I'm right, I have a feeling the colors won't last."

"Oh, what a shame."

Jessie heard the sound of running water and the chinking of the teapot from the kitchen.

She unfastened the safety pin from the waist of her dress and held it out.

"Here's your magic treasure back," she said with a grin. "And Emerald sends her love and thanks."

Granny's eyebrows rose even higher.

"We *do* have a lot to talk about," she said. "But before we do, go and look in your room. There are some presents for you there. I found them in the pine glade just now when I went down to pick up the red umbrella."

Jessie ran to her bedroom. Sure enough, on her dressing table there was the little basket Dawn had given her, filled with all the other pixies' "gifties." There was a note, too, but the printing was so tiny that Jessie couldn't read it.

She took her magnifying glass from her desk drawer and bent over the note.

DEER JESSIE,

WE ARE SORY YOU GOT BLONE AWAY. HEER ARE YOUR GIFTIES AND ONE EXTRA FROM THE REALM FOKE. MAYBELLE SEZ DON'T WORRY. IT ONLY WERKS NEAR TOADSTOOLS. SEE YOU SOONE.

So Maybelle had visited the pixies to tell them Jessie was safe, as she had promised. Jessie wondered what the extra "giftie" could be.

She sorted through the things piled in the basket. There was something wrapped in silver paper. She opened the parcel carefully with a fingernail. Inside was a tiny slice of strawberry. Old Dingle had finished cutting up the birthday treat, and this was her share.

But beneath it was something else.

A tiny golden key.

It only works near toadstools, the note had said. Well, thank goodness for that, thought Jessie.

She fastened the little key to her charm bracelet, and looked at it.

She remembered the laughing, funny pixies.

The terrifying rush as she was blown through the air by the fierce wind. The monster parrot flying toward the rainbow. The rainbow fairies' voices, chiming through the color mists. Emerald's sad eyes beginning to glow with joy. Her Realm friends rushing up the palace stairs.

"Thank you, Granny," she whispered. "Thank you, pixies. Thank you, parrot. Thank you, rainbow fairies. Thank you, Maybelle, Giff, Patrice, Queen Helena . . ."

Through her open window she thought she heard tiny voices calling.

"Many happies, Jessie."

Jessie touched the golden key and smiled. She would have many other birthdays, she knew. But this was one she would never forget.

Turn the page for a peek at
Jessie's next adventure in the

Fairy Realm:

BOOK 6

The Unicorn

Jessie woke just before dawn. She wasn't sure what had woken her. She sat up in bed and shivered. It was cold. Very cold. And she felt uneasy—as though something was wrong.

She listened, but Blue Moon was silent. There wasn't a sound anywhere in the old house. Everything was dark and still. She shivered again. The breeze coming through her bedroom window was icy.

"There's snow about," Granny had said the night before, as Jessie's mother, Rosemary, added a log to the crackling fire in the living room. "I'd say there'll be a fall tonight or tomorrow. Just in time for the Festival."

Remembering this, Jessie turned quickly to look out into the garden. It was still dark but she could see that there was no snow outside. Just frost, white and hard, icing the grass.

Maybe it'll snow later, thought Jessie. Oh, I hope it does.

She lay down again and cuddled deep under

her quilt. It was Saturday, the day of the Winter Festival. This afternoon she was singing with the school choir at a concert in the town hall. Afterward there would be a barbecue and fireworks and dancing in the park.

Jessie knew it was going to be a tiring day. She should get some more sleep. But somehow she didn't feel like sleeping at all. That strange fearful feeling was still with her. Even the thought of snow hadn't driven it away.

Jessie closed her eyes and lay still, trying to let her mind drift. She used all the ways she knew to make herself slip back into sleep.

She counted slowly to a hundred. Then she tried to think of things that made her feel happy and peaceful. She thought of her mother, and Granny, and Granny's big ginger cat, Flynn, all fast asleep in their beds. And, of course, she thought of the magical world of the Realm.

No one but Jessie and her grandmother knew about the invisible Door at the bottom of the Blue Moon garden. No one else knew about the enchanting fairy world beyond. Jessie had discovered them both by accident. But of course Granny had known about them all her life.

Snuggled under the covers, her eyes tightly closed, Jessie smiled. It was still so amazing to think that her own grandmother had been born in the Realm. That she was its rightful Queen, but had left it, long ago, to marry Robert Belairs, the human man she loved.

Robert had lived at Blue Moon. He'd discovered the secret Door. During his life he'd become famous for his wonderful paintings of the Realm.

Of course, everyone thought Robert Belairs had just imagined these magical fairy scenes that appeared in so many books, and hung in art galleries all over the world. But Jessie knew her grandfather had painted things he'd really seen. Fairies and elves. Mermaids and unicorns and miniature horses. Gnomes, pixies, and dwarfs. And so much more.

Jessie thought about all the extraordinary things she herself had seen and done since she had found the secret Door. She thought about all her Realm friends, especially Maybelle the miniature horse, Giff, the elf, and Patrice, the palace housekeeper.

On the table beside her bed lay Jessie's charm bracelet. Every charm had been given to her by the Folk of the Realm, to remind her of her Realm adventures. As if she could ever forget. How could anyone forget such magical, exciting times?

Jessie knew she was very lucky to have found the Realm. And she was very lucky to have such a special grandmother.

Her thoughts drifted on. What would her friends think, if they knew? To them, Granny was just Mrs. Jessica Belairs of Blue Moon. Jessie's grandmother. Rosemary's mother. A widow now, since Jessie's grandfather had died. An old lady with sparkling green eyes, white hair, and a soft, laughing voice.

They didn't know how special she was. But everyone loved her. Except, of course . . .

EMILY RODDA

has written many books for children, including the Rowan of Rin books. She has won the Children's Book Council of Australia Book of the Year Award an unprecedented five times. A former editor, Ms. Rodda is also the best-selling author of adult mysteries under the name Jennifer Rowe. She lives in Australia.